If Kids Ruled the World

For all the kids who'd like to go
to Recess School — L.B.

For my kids and all my nieces and
nephews, who will surely take over
the world — D.H.

Text © 2014 Linda Bailey
Illustrations © 2014 David Huyck

Kids Can Press acknowledges the financial support of the Government of
Ontario, through the Ontario Media Development Corporation's Ontario Book
Initiative; the Ontario Arts Council; the Canada Council for the Arts; and the
Government of Canada, through the CBF, for our publishing activity.

Published in Canada by
Kids Can Press Ltd.
25 Dockside Drive
Toronto, ON M5A 0B5

Published in the U.S. by
Kids Can Press Ltd.
2250 Military Road
Tonawanda, NY 14150

www.kidscanpress.com

The artwork in this book was rendered digitally.
The text is set in Minya Nouvelle.

Edited by Tara Walker and Debbie Rogosin
Designed by Julia Naimska

This book is smyth sewn casebound.
Manufactured in Shenzhen, China, in 4/2014 by C & C Offset

CM 14 0 9 8 7 6 5 4 3 2 1

Library and Archives Canada Cataloguing in Publication

Bailey, Linda, 1948-, author
        If kids ruled the world / written by Linda Bailey ; illustrated
by David Huyck.

ISBN 978-1-55453-591-0 (bound)

        I. Huyck, David, 1976-, illustrator II. Title.

PS8553.A3644I45 2014   jC813'.54   C2011-904469-2

Kids Can Press is a Corus™ Entertainment company

If Kids Ruled the World

Written by Linda Bailey

Illustrated by David Huyck

KIDS CAN PRESS

If kids ruled the world,
every day would be your birthday!

Birthday cake would be **good** for you.

Your doctor would say,
"Don't forget to eat your birthday cake
so you'll grow up strong and healthy!"

If kids ruled the world,
there'd be no such thing as bedtime.

Beds would be for bouncing on
and hiding underneath.

Pillows would be for pillow fights!

No one would ever **make** a bed.
What's the use of that?

If kids ruled the world,
the monster in your closet
would be scared of **you**!

Any time you wanted,
you could sneak up and yell,
"BOO!"

You'd hear a scream.
Then a thump.

That would be your monster ...
fainting!

You could wear anything you like.

A T-shirt.
A tutu.
A tuxedo.

You could even wear your underwear
on your head!

(Not that you'd **want** to.)

If you felt like going somewhere,
you'd have your own thingamajiggy to get there.

You could have a thingama-cycle
or a thingama-copter
or a thinga-balloon.

If you wanted to travel a **long** way,
you could take a pirate ship.

And if you wanted to travel a really long way ...

5, 4, 3, 2, 1 — BLAST OFF!

You could have all the pets you like.
Any kind!

A kangaroo.
An elephant.
A grizzly bear.

Well ... maybe not a grizzly bear.

Every prince would have a castle,
and so would every princess.

And **everyone** could be a prince or princess!

Every yard would have a lake

with frogs for catching
and rafts for riding,
a dock for diving
and a mysterious island
to swim to ...

And what would you find
if you followed a map?

X marks the spot for treasure!

You'd never have to take a bath again.
That's what the **lake** is for.

But if you felt like taking a bath ...

... you could have all the bubbles
you wanted, and a bathtub big
enough for **all** your friends!

Every yard would have a tree.
Every tree would have a tree house.
And every tree house would have
a rope ladder to pull up behind.

You could keep your
secret diary there.
Your secret codes, too.
You wouldn't even
have to use invisible ink
because no one could come in.

Not unless **YOU** said so!

You could go to any kind of school you like ...

Circus School.

Fairy School.

Inventing School.

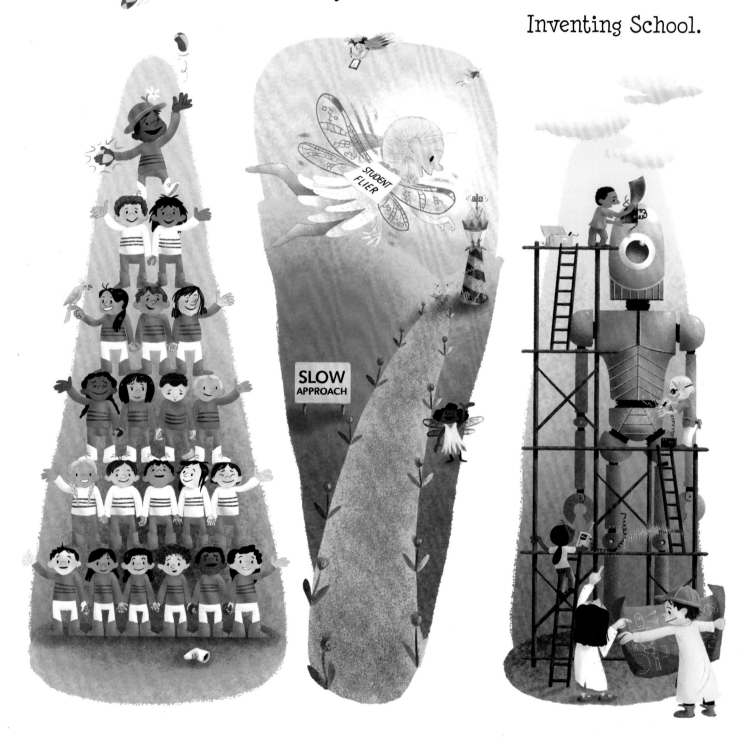

Lots of kids would
go to Recess School.

If kids ruled the world,
all the sidewalks would be trampolines ...

all the cars would be ponies ...

and dinosaurs would live in the park.

And no one would ever forget how to
PLAY!

No way!

Not even if they turned
a hundred and six years old
and lost all their teeth.

There'd be plenty of **play** for everyone ...

if **kids** ruled the world.